Enchanted Stories

The Elves & the Shoemaker

Once there was a shoemaker who was very poor. He only had enough material for one last pair of shoes. He laid out his tools and leather ready for the morning.

"Tomorrow I shall make my last pair of shoes and then what will we do?"

"Do not worry, my dear," said his wife. "We are good people. We shall find a way."

When the shoemaker awoke the very next morning, he couldn't believe his eyes. Sitting on his workbench was a beautiful pair of shoes!

He looked closer and saw that the shoes were put together perfectly, with every single stitch in the right place! The shoemaker and his wife didn't know what to think. Suddenly, there was a knock at the door.

The shoemaker opened it to see a man standing outside.
"My shoes are worn out," said the man. "Can you sell me a new pair."

So, the shoemaker showed the customer the brand new pair of shoes.
The customer loved them and they fitted him perfectly! He paid the
shoemaker a handsome price for the shoes.

With the money he had earned, the shoemaker went out and bought the
materials he needed to make two more pairs of shoes.

Once again, when he woke the next morning, there, sitting on the
workbench, were two brand new pairs of shoes!

The shoemaker and his wife were astonished. Who on earth could have
made these wonderful shoes?

Then, once again they heard a knock at the door. They opened it to two men. They said, "Our good friend visited us yesterday wearing the most glorious shoes we have ever seen!" We simply had to come and see for ourselves the shop that sells these shoes!"

So, the shoemaker showed the customers in. They tried on the new shoes, and once again they fitted perfectly. This time the customers paid double! The shoemaker once again bought materials and got everything ready for the next day's work. Once more the shoes were all completed when he awoke and there were even more customers already waiting outside the shop!

Every shoe fitted every foot perfectly. The shoemaker made enough extra money to buy a wonderful meal for his wife along with the materials for the next day.

Just before they went to bed, the shoemaker's wife said, "My darling, we have been ever so fortunate to be blessed by whatever magic has made these shoes. Let us stay awake and watch what happens, and then maybe we can somehow thank whoever has been helping us."

So, the shoemaker and his wife stayed up and hid behind a big armchair in the corner of the room. They waited and waited and then suddenly, when the clock struck midnight, a dozen little elves came tumbling down the chimney!

The elves picked up the tools and the leather and began making the shoes. When all the work was done, the elves bounced back up the chimney, leaving behind some of the finest footwear the shoemaker had ever seen!

"We must do something for these elves," said the shoemaker's wife. The shoemaker thought about it for a moment then said, "Did you see their feet?" "Yes!" replied his wife. "They weren't wearing any shoes!"

"Perhaps I could make them new pairs of shoes?" said the shoemaker. "Yes! That's a wonderful idea!" said the shoemaker's wife. "Did you see those tatty old rags they were wearing? Well, I shall make them some beautiful new clothes to wear instead."

So, that very day, the shoemaker began making twelve little pairs of shoes while his wife made twelve fine shirts and twelve pairs of trousers.

That evening, the shoemaker left out twelve tiny outfits.

He left out twelve tiny pairs of shoes. The shoemaker and his wife hid behind the big armchair and waited for the elves to appear.

When midnight arrived, the elves came tumbling down the chimney and saw the beautiful presents that had been left for them.

The elves were ecstatic! They cheered and danced and then put
on their new shoes and one by one they jumped out of the window.

The shoemaker never saw the elves again. He went on to
be very successful and his shoes became well known in all the
fashionable cities. He never forgot the elves that helped him.

Snow White & Rose Red

Once upon a time, a poor widow lived with her two daughters. The girls were called Snow White and Rose Red.

One cold winter's evening, they were sitting beside the fire when there was a knock at the door. Rose Red ran to pull it open. "Aaaaahhhh!" she screamed. She was face to face with a big brown bear. "Do not be afraid. I won't hurt you," said the bear in a surprisingly gentle voice. "May I come in to warm myself beside your fire?" "Please do, you poor bear!" said the widow.

At first, Snow White and Rose Red were afraid of the big brown bear. Then, bit by bit, they became used to him. Before long, they were playing with him and having lots of fun.

For the rest of the winter, the bear was like one of the family. He slept beside the fire each night, and returned to the forest each day.

When spring arrived, the bear told the girls he had to go away. "I must guard my treasure from the wicked dwarfs who come out of their holes in the spring," he explained.

Later that day, Snow White and Rose Red were collecting firewood when they saw something dancing around a fallen tree.

It was an angry-looking dwarf with a long, jet-black beard.
His beard was trapped beneath the tree.
"What are you staring at?" he yelled at the girls.
"Why don't you help?"

The girls pulled and pulled, but they could not free the beard.
"Don't worry," said Snow White. "I will help you."

She pulled her scissors out of her pocket and snipped
his beard. As soon as the dwarf was free, he grabbed a bag of gold from
among the tree's roots and turned his back on the girls.
"Nasty girl, cutting off my fine beard," he hissed.

Shortly afterwards, Snow White and Rose Red were walking by the brook when they saw the dwarf again. A big fish had caught hold of his beard and was pulling him into the water. The two girls caught hold of the dwarf and tried to pull him free. The fish was just too strong, and the girls couldn't pull the dwarf free. Not knowing what else to do, Snow White pulled out her scissors and cut the beard.

"You toadstool!" screamed the dwarf once he was free. "Do you want to ruin all of my beautiful beard?" Then, without another word, he dragged a sack of pearls out of the reeds and disappeared.

A few days later, Snow White and Rose Red were walking to town when they heard someone scream.

They ran towards the noise and saw that a huge eagle had grabbed the bad-tempered dwarf.

"Quick," said Rose Red. Each girl grabbed one of the dwarf's legs. They pulled and pulled until the eagle finally let go.

The dwarf jumped to his feet and grabbed a bag of jewels.
"You clumsy creatures!" he snarled. "Couldn't you have been more careful? Look, my lovely coat is all torn."

By now, the girls were so used to the ungrateful dwarf's bad manners that they continued to town without giving him a further thought.

Later that evening, the girls were returning home when they saw something sparkling in the moonlight. The dwarf was pulling sacks of treasure out of a hole and spreading it out on the grass. It looked so lovely that the girls stopped to stare.

"What are you staring at?" screamed the dwarf in a rage.

He didn't stop shouting at them until there was a loud growl and the brown bear leaped out of the forest.

The bear sprang forward and cuffed the dwarf with a powerful paw.

The dwarf gave a yell and fell to the ground.

Meanwhile, the two girls had run away to hide.
"Come back, Snow White and Rose Red," called the bear in a
gentle voice.
"Don't be afraid. I won't hurt you."

It was Snow White's and Rose Red's friend.

They ran to hug him. When they did, the most surprising thing happened.
His bearskin fell away to reveal a handsome young man.

"I am Prince Levi," he said. "That wicked dwarf stole my treasure and turned me into a bear. I was doomed to live as a bear for as long as he lived."

As Snow White gazed into the prince's sea-blue eyes, her heart began to pound. She was falling in love. Luckily, Prince Levi felt exactly the same.

Not long afterwards, there was a huge wedding. Snow White married Prince Levi and Rose Red married his brother, Prince Sebastian.

They all lived happily ever after.

Thumbelina

Once there was a wife who longed for a little girl. So she went to see an old wise woman, to ask for her help.

The woman gave the wife a barley seed. "This is not like the seed the farmer sows," said the old woman. "This is a special seed, which you must take home and plant in a pot."

The wife took the seed and planted it. Soon, a beautiful yellow and red flower grew. The wife thought it so beautiful that she couldn't help kissing it. At once, the petals unfurled. There, in the middle, sat a delicate girl with golden hair. She was tiny, smaller even than a thumb, so the wife named her Thumbelina..

One night an ugly toad came hopping in through the window and saw Thumbelina asleep. "What a pretty wife she will make for my son," the toad said, and she picked up the bed, then hopped out of the window. She placed the bed on a water lily. "She cannot escape from here," thought the toad.

When Thumbelina awoke she began to cry.
"Dry your tears," croaked the toad. "You are to marry my son, and you shall live together in the mud."

The toad's son was very ugly and poor Thumbelina did not want to marry him. "Who will save me now?" she sobbed.

Luckily, the fish in the stream felt sorry for the beautiful girl.
When the toad was sleeping, they chewed the stem of the lily leaf on which Thumbelina sat. At once, the flowing water carried Thumbelina and the leaf off down stream, far away from the ugly toads.

She was just beginning to feel happy again, when suddenly a large beetle buzzed down, seized her and flew high into a tree.

"How pretty you are," the beetle told the tiny girl. "Would you like some honey?" It wasn't long before the other lady beetles heard about the tiny girl, and came to see Thumbelina for themselves.

"She only has two legs. How ugly!" laughed one, giving
Thumbelina a prod.
"Look! She has no feelers," cried another. "How odd!"

Embarrassed by their laughter, the male beetle picked up the tiny girl and
set her down on a daisy in the field below.

All summer and autumn Thumbelina lived in the wood. When winter
arrived it grew very cold. She walked through the wood until she came to
a hole where a field mouse lived. Thumbelina knocked on the door.

When the kindly mouse saw the little girl, she was filled with pity.
"Come in, child," she said. "You must be frozen."

The mouse listened in silence as Thumbelina told her story.
Then she smiled. "Why don't you come and live with me?" she suggested,
smiling. So, Thumbelina stayed with the mouse. One day the mouse told
Thumbelina that her friend the, mole would be visiting.
"He is most handsome," she said. "He would make you a fine husband."

When the mole arrived, he took quite a fancy to Thumbelina.
"This is a passage between my home and yours," he said, showing
Thumbelina a dark tunnel. "You are most welcome to use it to visit me
anytime. Do be careful there is a dead bird in there."

Thumbelina looked into the tunnel. There on the floor lay a
dead swallow. When she saw the poor bird, tears filled her eyes. "I will
bring him a cover," she whispered, stroking its feathers.

As Thumbelina placed the cover over the swallow, she was surprised to
feel his heart beating. The tiny girl was filled with joy. The bird
was alive!

All through the long winter, Thumbelina cared for the swallow. Finally,
when spring arrived, Thumbelina knew her friend was strong enough to
fly once more.

"It's time for you to leave," said Thumbelina bravely. She made a hole in the roof of the tunnel so the swallow could escape.

"Why don't you come with me," said the swallow. But Thumbelina could not leave the mouse after all her kindness, so she gave the bird one last hug, then watched as her friend flew away.

That night, the mole asked Thumbelina to marry him. Although she did not want to, Thumbelina agreed, just to make the mouse happy.

Finally, the day came when the mole came to fetch his wife and take her deep into his dark hole. Thumbelina thought her heart might break in two. Suddenly, the swallow flew by. Thumbelina told him all about the mole and his dark, dark hole.

"Come with me," said the swallow. "I am flying to a place where the sun always shines." Thumbelina flew with the swallow far away to a warm country.

The swallow landed gently on the petals of a flower. Inside the flower was a tiny young man. Thumbelina instantly fell in love with him.

"I am the King of the flower spirits," said the tiny man. He fell in love with Thumbelina and asked her to be his queen. Thumbelina was very happy. At last she had found her true home.